A Friend

Zea Perez

Ukiyoto Publishing

All global publishing rights are held by

Ukiyoto Publishing

Published in 2024

Content Copyright © Zea Perez

ISBN 9789362690364

All rights reserved.

No part of this publication may be reproduced, transmitted, or stored in a retrieval system, in any form by any means, electronic, mechanical, photocopying, recording or otherwise, without the prior permission of the publisher.

The moral rights of the authors have been asserted.

This is a work of fiction. Names, characters, businesses, places, events, locales, and incidents are either the products of the author's imagination or used in a fictitious manner. Any resemblance to actual persons, living or dead, or actual events is purely coincidental.

This book is sold subject to the condition that it shall not by way of trade or otherwise, be lent, resold, hired out or otherwise circulated, without the publisher's prior consent, in any form of binding or cover other than that in which it is published.

www.ukiyoto.com

Dedication

My deepest gratitude to Ukiyoto and to the Editing Team for trusting that my children's tales are worth publishing and equally worth reading.

To my family and 'monk kids', Mama Sabel and Papa Jr ShayneMon&hisDad; and the whole happy bunch fam IsayPengJangTin; and to MomDaAdi&Lesu's and MomDadNitz fam VirMacMar, thank you for believing and giving me the necessary space, time and assistance to pursue my passion in writing.

To Momshie Ma'am Rachel in her spirit and to her family, my sincere gratitude. My books are for you. I know your heart melts with children. I've written a lot of children's tales when we were together and shall continue writing with you as a guiding inspiration.

To Pretty wife and her hubby, thank you for bestowing me the fastest internet connection; and to Mr. and Mrs. Magno for the lovely abode- ideal for writing, to the siblings: Owen, Roelaiza, and Rossan - many thanks for all the instant help and domestic relief and tales. Your kindness is etched here in my heart;

To Giulietta, thank you, for being so kind to read, to share your thoughts and for writing endorsement quotes; your recommendations about the content are very significant on improving the book.

To sir Paul R Stanton, thank you for reading and for giving your honest critique. They are relevant and enriching.

To Jae Oh, for being so accommodating to read and edit initially the story.

To Aoi and Vnius for the hearts, they are very encouraging.

My heartwarming embrace of gratefulness to Mama S, a septuagenarian, a living inspiration who revealed to me her fantastic tales about nature, her life and struggle as a woman and as a person. I hope we can find time soon to write your stories with memories of your hometown's beautiful landscapes.

To Ma'am Fe and sir Gen, thank you very much for being so kind to support my subsistence as a children's writer thru projects you entrusted. Also, thank you to Ma'am Ofel, Ma'am Lerma and Ma'am Rose for the support.

My immense and bottomless thanks to my family-like friends:

To sir Marlou, who is always kind to extend a helping hand, rain or shine. Your time shared is priceless and a treasure to keep!

To sir Nico, Mommy Luz and family for the short yet restful vacation;

To sir Joel, his wife Ma'am Jen and to their kids-Mikee and Little Girl Tela, I treasure every moment we bond together, your care, love and support are revitalizing!

To Ma'am Sharmaine, my new captured reader, who gave all her honest opinion about the tale.

To Ma'am Liwa my 'ever captured' reader, her husband and beautiful children, it is such a lovely thing having you around as my neighbor and family;

To sir Rowel, who lent his creativity for the making and critique of the cover designs; for comfortably telling me his coming of age and inspiring stories, and for his endless patience and support in all spheres; for giving me relief through difficult times, they are too many to mention!

To sir Charlie and Ma'am Millie for believing in my creativity and for looking after my welfare;

Most of all, my enormous appreciation to my ever harsh, ever gentle editor and reader JEC and to his family. We share the love for children and their antics, hence these stories. The tales have become tight, silkier and more fun to read because of your skillful, intense yet funny and nurturing critique and editing.

I dedicate this book to the kids who asked and said 'What is to be my place under the sun?' and 'Nobody loves me, I'm just a poor kid!'; To BH Three Seven always an inspiration; to Nippy a selfless soul and with a big heart; and to the children of today and the next generation to come.

Zea Perez

When Dad comes home from work, he brings with him a present for Kaloy. It is a huge basket with a cloth cover wrapped around it.

'Mom, Dad is here!' Kaloy shouts and welcomes his dad with a big hug.

Mom comes from the bedroom where she has laid baby Kai for his afternoon nap. She smiles at Dad and kisses him on the cheek.

Dad hangs the basket on the clothes line in the corner of the balcony.

Dad says, 'Kaloy, remember when you asked about having a cat as a pet? And Mom said maybe you should have a different pet because cats, like dogs, are hairy and cause her to suffer an allergic reaction.'

'Yes Dad, I remember,' Kaloy replies.

'Now your wish to have a pet-friend is granted,' Dad says, smiling.
'It has feathers and no hairs,' Mom says.
Dad and Mom open the cloth covering of the basket.

Kaloy's eyes widen.

He recognizes the basket is really a cage - a plastic, brown bird cage!

Inside is a perching, colourful, little bird. Its wings have the tint of dark green and a splash of yellow and orange. Its beak is beige and its eyes appear so round in the dark feathers of its face.

Kaloy smiles and asks, 'What's the name of the bird, Mom, Dad?'

'It has no name yet. The pet shop owner said the bird is a girl. What would you like to call her, Kaloy?' Dad asks.

'Let's call her Twit,' Kaloy responds.

'That's a cute name,' Mom says.

'Twit it is!' Dad approves.

Taking Good Care of a Friend

Dad shows Kaloy how to take care of the bird. Kaloy learns that Twit loves bananas and berries for food.

He is shown how to put water in the little container for Twit to drink when she becomes thirsty inside her cage.

A FRIEND

'Hello, Twit!' Kaloy greets the bird.
'Tweet! Tweet!' the bird answers.
'Are you happy today?'
The bird hops excitedly. 'Tweet! Tweet!'
Kaloy laughs and hops too.

Twit Grows Bigger

A year later, Twit has grown bigger. She can flap her wings wider.

With her sturdier feet, she can walk, hop and jump more easily. She can finish a serving of banana quickly with her strong beak!

Kaloy enjoys watching the bird play with a little ball by rolling it with her beak. He is so happy when talking with Twit, as the bird responds to him with a loud 'Twit! Twit! Twit' while flapping her wings.

A Beautiful Friend in The Sky

One morning as Kaloy is about to feed the bird with her banana meal, he observes that she is quiet.

Concerned, Kaloy asks, 'How are you Twit?'

A FRIEND

The bird stays still.

'Are you sick?'

Twit continues being silent and moves into one corner of the cage.

She stares in the direction of a coconut tree, which grows across from the family's balcony.

Kaloy looks in the same direction and sees another bird perched on the tree!

A FRIEND

'Tweet! Tweet!' the bird calls from the coconut tree.
'Is it a friend of yours, Twit?' Kaloy asks his pet friend.
'Tweet! Tweet!' Twit keeps staring at the other bird.

A FRIEND

Kaloy suddenly recalls a story Mom and Dad have often read to him, about a little bird who dreams of flying. He remembers hearing that birds are happier when they are free in the open sky where they can flap their wings and fly as far and wide as they wish.

Kaloy goes immediately to Mom and Dad.

'What is it, Kaloy?' Mom asks.

'Can I release Twit from its cage?'

'Why do you want to let it go, Kaloy?' Dad asks.

A FRIEND

'Because just now I observed Twit was sad and began flapping her wings when she saw her bird friend!' Kaloy points through the window to show Mom and Dad the bird on the coconut tree.

'Besides,' Kaloy continues, 'I learned from the book we read that birds are happier when they can fly freely.'

'I see. How clever of you to recall the tale,' Mom says.

A FRIEND

At once, Dad, Mom and Kaloy go to the balcony together to look at the pet bird. Twit stares back at them.

Kaloy opens the door of the cage and says:

'Come out, Twit! It's time for you to fly!'

Twit comes forward from the back of the cage.

'It's time to explore the world, Twit!' says Dad, handing the bird over to his son.

Kaloy holds the bird lightly with both hands and, slowly opening his fingers, he gently frees the bird into the air.

Twit flaps her wings and flies up to the coconut tree to be with her friend.

'Tweet! Tweet! Tweet!' the birds call together.

From the top of the tree, they flap their wings and together take off into the air. Once in the air, they glide like little airplanes.

Twit and her friend fly by the balcony and call loudly to Kaloy and his parents, as if to say 'Thank you' and 'Goodbye'.

'Twit is more beautiful to watch in the sky than in her cage, Mom!' Kaloy says.

'Indeed, Kaloy! Indeed!' Mom replies. 'I suppose all creatures are much happier living outside cages than inside.'

Kaloy smiles at Mom and continues to watch Twit and her bird friend soar across the clear, blue sky.

About the Author

Zea Perez

Zea Perez is passionate to write about tales and verses especially dedicated to children. She weaves stories with themes manifesting about empowering children and love for Mother Nature. Writing and reading crystallize her thoughts and pave ways for her to ponder meaningful life perspectives. She has a terrace garden she tends every day.

Some of her pieces are published on flashfictionnorth, InkPantry, Literaryard, Twist and Twain, AllPoetry and shortkidstories, among others.

She is a top and trusted book reviewer of Coffee and Thorn Book Tour and Promotion. She writes book reviews for Goodreads, Amazon and other review platforms. A self-sustaining author - she works as a part-time content writer, proofreader, illustrator and a digital graphic artist.

Her books warmly find its home in Ukiyoto Publishing, namely – 'THE EIGHTH WONDER' (2022); 'GUARDIANS OF MOTHER EARTH' – A COLLECTION OF TALES (2022); 'GROWING UP

WITH KALOY' – A COLLECTION OF STORIES (2022); 'THE KIND MOON AND THE HARDWORKING SUN' (2023); 'A SATURDAY' (2023); 'A LOVELY TUNE' (2023); 'A NEW YEAR'S EVE' (2023); 'A FRIEND' (2024)